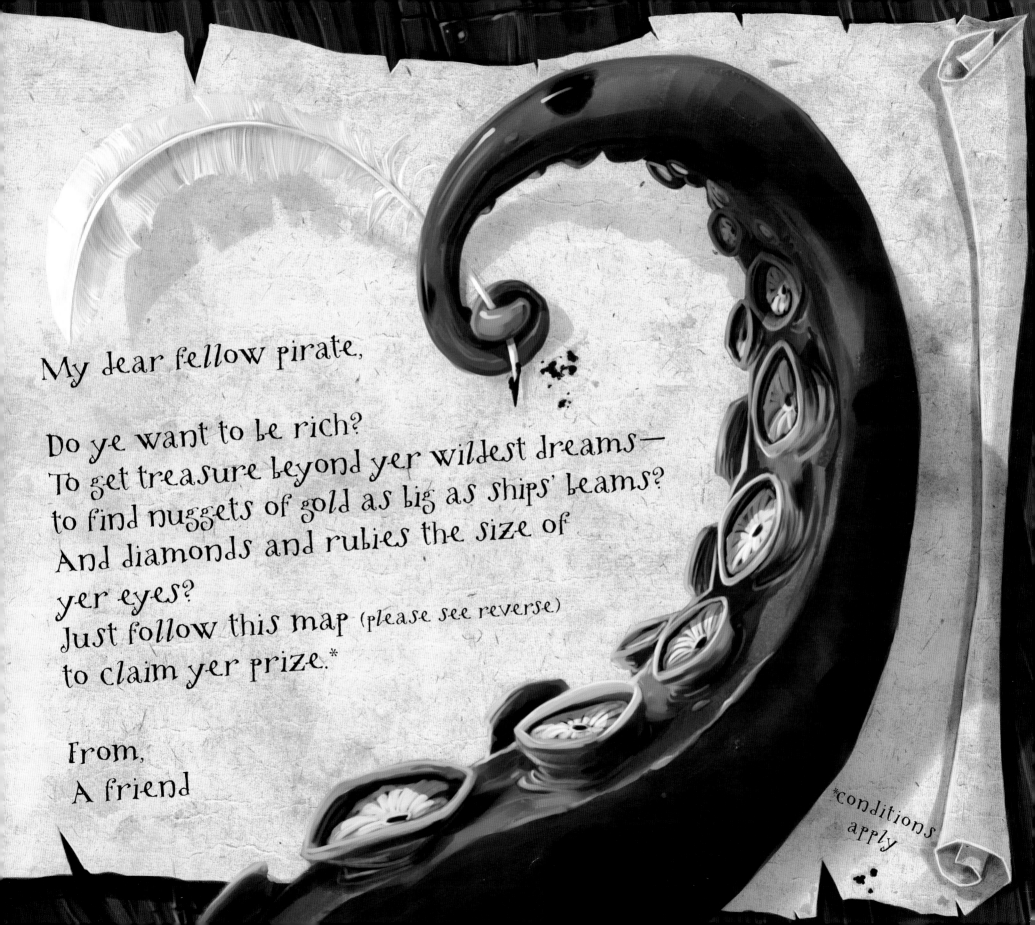

My dear fellow pirate,

Do ye want to be rich?
To get treasure beyond yer wildest dreams—
to find nuggets of gold as big as ships' beams?
And diamonds and rubies the size of
yer eyes?
Just follow this map (please see reverse)
to claim yer prize.*

From,
A friend

*conditions apply

For Dad, because I know
you would have been proud

First U.S. edition 2010

Library of Congress Cataloging-in-Publication Data is available.
Library of Congress Catalog Card Number pending
ISBN 978-0-7636-4876-3

10 11 12 13 TLF 10 9 8 7 6 5 4 3 2

Printed in Dongguan, Guangdong, China

This book was typeset in Aunt Mildred and Tree Boxelder.
The illustrations were done in digital media.

Edited by Libby Hamilton

templar books
an imprint of Candlewick Press
99 Dover Street
Somerville, Massachusetts 02144
www.candlewick.com

THE PIRATE CRUNCHER

JONNY DUDDLE

All was unusually quiet
in Port Royal . . .

but if you listened carefully, on the docks,

down the alleyways,
and in the candlelit taverns,

Thirsty Parrot

you could hear the
faint sound of a fiddle
floating on the wind.

Outside the Thirsty Parrot Inn, an old fiddler appeared. As he fiddled, he sang a song:

"I WAS SAILING ONE DAY AND WHAT DID I SEE?
AN ISLAND OF GOLD IN THE SCURVY SEA!
WITH A FIDDLE-DE-DEE,
THERE'LL BE TREASURE FOR ME.
FIDDLE-DE-DEE, ACROSS THE SEA."

His chantey caught the ear of the dastardly Captain Purplebeard, who bellowed out the window . . .

To the captain's delight, the fiddler replied,

'AS I SAILED THE SEAS, I SCRIBBLED A MAP,
SO THAT WHEN I GOT HOME, I COULD FIND MY
WAY BACK. YE CANNOT IMAGINE THE BOOTY
THAT'S THERE—A HUGE
HAUL OF TREASURE
BEYOND COMPARE!'

Ha-
HaRRR!

"I can imagine a shipload of
treasure!" roared Captain Purplebeard.
"Diamonds and rubies and gold
beyond measure. . . ."

The fiddler unfurled
his map and sang:

'I'LL SHOW YE MY MAP
IF YE'LL TAKE ME THERE—
THERE'LL BE TREASURE
ENOUGH FOR US ALL
TO SHARE!'

The sun was coming up
as Captain Purplebeard and
his cutthroat crew boarded
their ship, the BLACK HOLE.
Behind them came the
old fiddler, still dancing
and singing:

"TO FIND THIS ISLAND,
YOU'LL HAVE TO BE QUICK—
FOR THEY SAY IT PERFORMS
A VANISHING TRICK!
AND NONE WHO'VE TRIED
TO SET FOOT ON ITS SANDS
HAVE EVER RETURNED
TO PIRATE LANDS."

But the captain just sneered,
"What nonsense, I say."

So off they sailed across the sea.
And as they sat down to breakfast, the old fiddler began again:

"THERE IS ONE SMALL THING I FORGOT YESTERDAY—
THERE'S ALSO A MONSTER, OR SO THEY SAY,
THAT LIKES TO EAT PIRATES WHO COME FOR THE TREASURE,
AND CHEW UP THEIR SHIPS,
JUST FOR GOOD MEASURE."

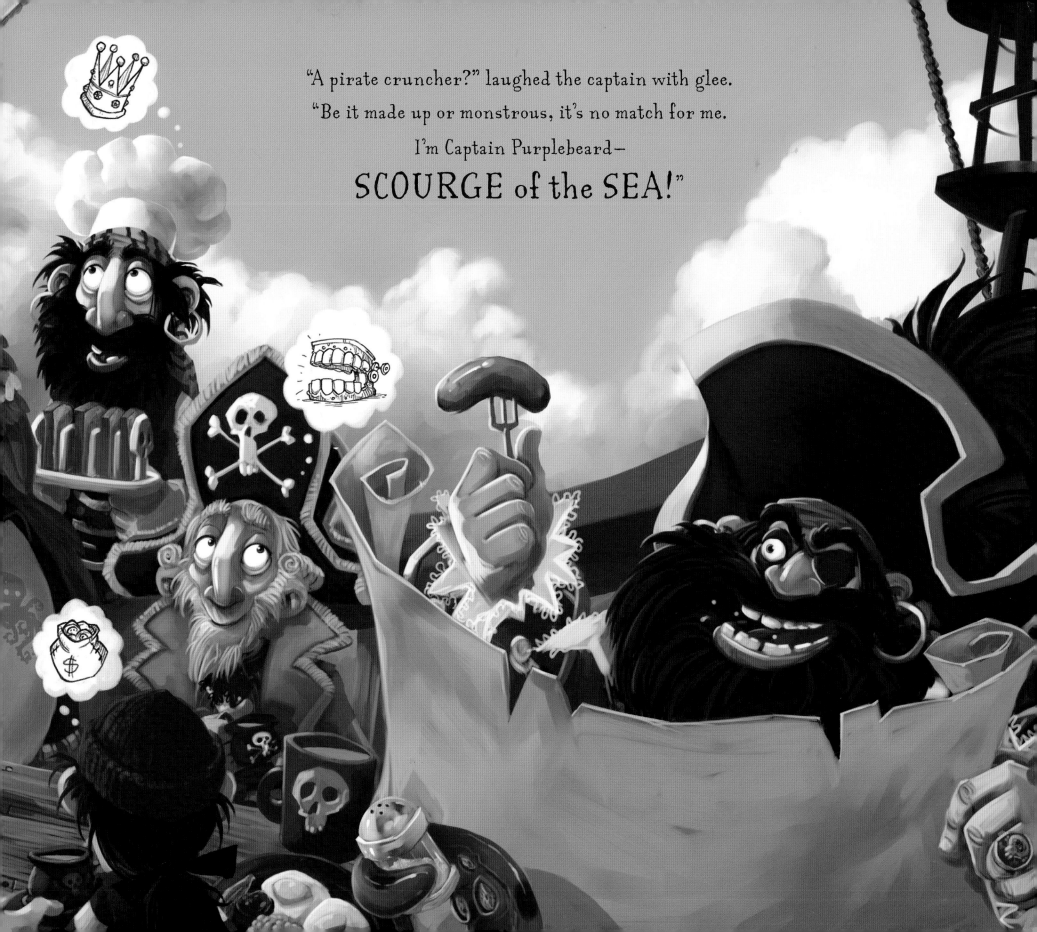

"A pirate cruncher?" laughed the captain with glee.
"Be it made up or monstrous, it's no match for me.
I'm Captain Purplebeard—
SCOURGE of the SEA!"

And the fiddler said:

'OH, YES, I AGREE.
IT DOESN'T SCARE ME!
NO, SIREE . . .

THOUGH, NO BONES ABOUT IT,
IT'S A BIG OLD BEAST,

THAT LIKES NOTHING MORE THAN A PIRATE FEAST.

IT CAN SWALLOW WHOLE SHIPS IN ITS WHIRLPOOL JAWS (THOUGH THEY SAY IT'S ALLERGIC TO SCARLET MACAWS)."

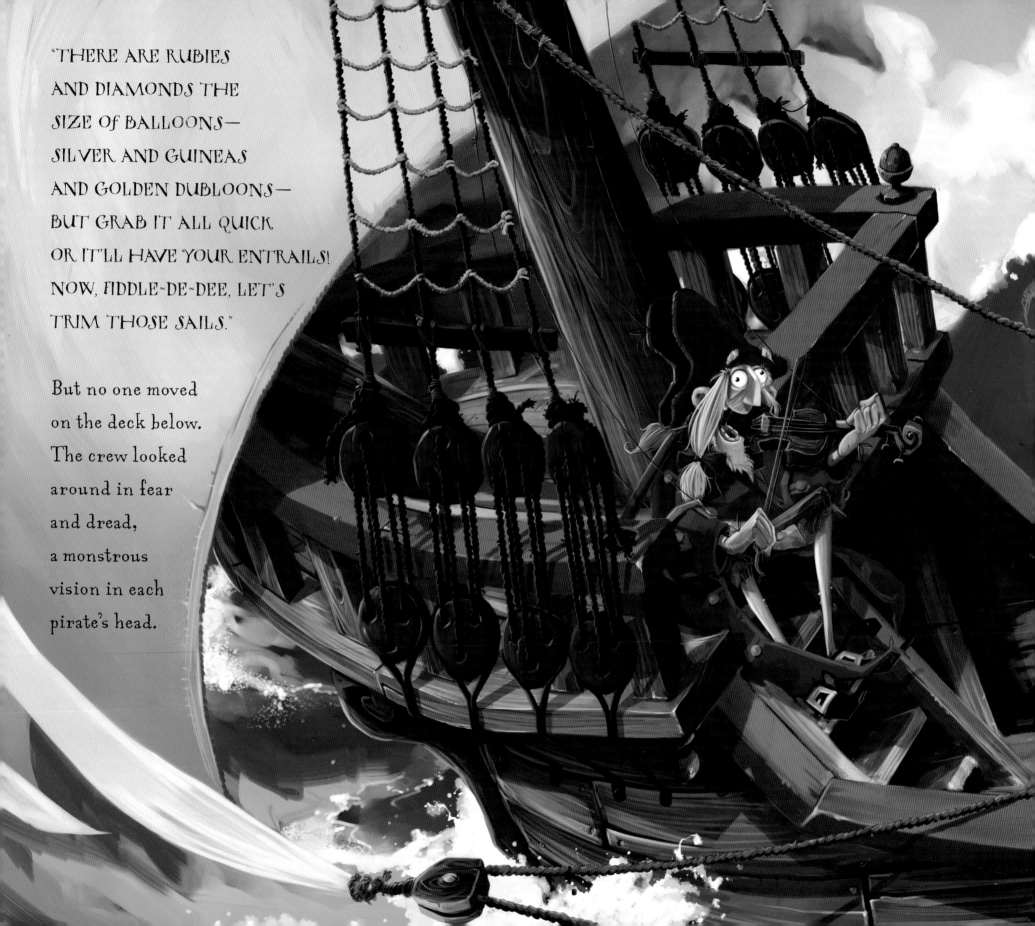

"THERE ARE RUBIES
AND DIAMONDS THE
SIZE OF BALLOONS—
SILVER AND GUINEAS
AND GOLDEN DUBLOONS—
BUT GRAB IT ALL QUICK
OR IT'LL HAVE YOUR ENTRAILS!
NOW, FIDDLE~DE~DEE, LET'S
TRIM THOSE SAILS."

But no one moved
on the deck below.
The crew looked
around in fear
and dread,
a monstrous
vision in each
pirate's head.

"Go home?"
roared Captain Purplebeard.
"Any cowardly landlubbers
will be tossed in the sea.
The only thing you should
be scared of is me!"

So with visions of monsters in every head,
the motley old crew trudged off to bed.
Most had nightmares and terrible dreams,
and the hold was full of pirate screams.

But on deck the captain just chortled with pleasure
for his head was stuffed full of dreams about treasure.
"Gold or silver, I don't care which,
just as long as it makes me filthy rich!"

The next morning, the crew couldn't be sure, but the day before it seemed that they had numbered one more.

And the fiddler told them:
'IF YOU'RE TOO SCARED, YOU CAN TURN
BACK TO PORT, WHILE YOU'RE STILL HEALTHY,
SAVE FOR SCURVY AND WARTS.
IT WOULD BE SAFER BY FAR
TO RETURN TO THE SHORE,
AND AS FOR THE TREASURE,
DO YOU REALLY
NEED MORE?'

"Shiver me timbers!" Captain Purplebeard laughed.
"You should know by now that never, ever
can any pirate have enough treasure.
And if there's a beast, it better beware.
I can smell that gold! We're almost there!"

Just then, from up in the crow's nest, there came a call.

LAND AHOY!

"HURRAH!" yelled the pirates, forgetting their fear, now that the promise of treasure was near.

As they clambered ashore,
no one saw a thing wrong –
too busy to heed
the fiddler's
last song.

'I WAS SWIMMING ONE DAY
AND WHAT DID I SEE?
A PIRATE~PACKED BOAT
IN THE SCURVY SEA!
WITH A FIDDLE~DE~DEE,
THERE'LL BE DINNER FOR ME.
FIDDLE~DE~DEE, ACROSS THE—"

Lubbers' Land

St. Andrew

Clarendon

The Blu...

St. David

Inner Harbor

Port Royal

Bull Bay

Galleon Harbor

Half Moon Bay

Cow Bay

Cutlass Point

Fiddle Bay

Carmine's Head

Monkey Bay

Scurvy Sands

Wreck Bay

Grundy Head

Butler Bay

Fish Head

Greasy Head

Peak Bay

There Be
TREASURE
Abroad!

oooOoo-AaaARR!

Ye Wavy Bit . . .